DATE DUE

APR 1 3 2000			
GAYLORD			PRINTED IN U.S.A.

Disney's MAGIC EYE™

3D Illusions by N.E. Thing Enterprises

MAGIC EYE

Andrews and McMeel
A Universal Press Syndicate Company
Kansas City

HYPERION

New York

Co-published by Hyperion, 114 Fifth Avenue, New York, New York 10011 and Andrews and McMeel, a Universal Press Syndicate Company, 4900 Main Street, Kansas City, Missouri 64112.

ISBN: 0-8362-7020-7

INTRODUCTION

It has been four short years since N.E. Thing Enterprises was first created with the (then) mad idea that "Magic Eye" pictures could find an audience. Even more amazing is the fact that the original MAGIC EYE book was first published in the United States less than a year ago. The skyrocket ride we've been on during the past year makes our knees weak, and, all too often, our weekends short. Of all the praise and reward passed our way in that time, none could really compare with the opportunity to work with the fabulous Walt Disney artists to create this book!

From the Magic Kingdom to the Magic Eye, Disney has always represented the highest standards in inventing fantasies and marvelous worlds which take us all to the kid's place in our hearts! Innovation, imagination, and technical creativity have always given their miracles that special Disney sense of ease and polish. It has been a wondrous array of shiny, glistening bubble worlds filled with flying elephants, sleeping princesses, and chattering chipmunks. And now, for the first time, in your hands is a book full of some of our most cherished Disney images, given a new dose of wonder and magic with the Magic Eye techniques that are sweeping the whole globe!

Combining these classic Disney scenes, some as brand-new as *The Lion King* and some we remember loving as children, with the computer-generated 3D wizardry of N.E. Thing Enterprises took a special kind of cooperation and care. I would like to thank Russell Schroeder, Jim Huser, and Tim Lewis of The Walt Disney Company for their incredible support and creative direction.

Our own Cheri Smith, with her unparalleled sense of design and color, has used her many talents to bring a new dimension to your Disney favorites. Soar with the Darlings off to Never Land or look through Belle's eyes into the heart of the Beast! You will see that which you never could before! Without Cheri's unlimited energy and dedication to perfection, this collaboration could not have come to fruition.

The very talented Andy Paraskevas's hand can be seen throughout this book; from the lovable Pumbaa to the elegance of Cinderella, Andy will guide you to new depths of vision!

And we must not forget Eileen Kenneally, of "Kenneally Creative," whose Wizzy Nodwig character graces the end pages of this otherwise totally Disney book. Wizzy was born out of the collaboration between N.E. Thing Enterprises and Eileen, and her multitude of talents which brought him to life. His boundless optimism and sense of whimsy come from her side of the family!

Special recognition is certainly deserved by the amazing Magic Eye techniques developed by Bohdan Petyhyrycz and Peter Ciavarella of Digi-Rule Inc. of Calgary, Alberta, Canada. Please take a close look at the image of Pluto on page 22 and marvel at his fully dimensioned face. Quite a job, Bohdan! We at N.E. Thing Enterprises have formed a strategic partnership with Digi-Rule to create an ever more amazing 3D world for you. So keep your eyes wide for more and more amazing Magic Eye marvels in coming months and years!

This most incredible collaboration has come to pass because of the limitless talents of the creative staffs at both Disney and N.E. Thing Enterprises, but is finally made possible only by you, the "reader." It is with great pride and pleasure that we present this book to all of you who helped us turn the phrase "3D" into a verb.

VIEWING TECHNIQUES

Learning to use your MAGIC EYE is a bit like learning to ride a bicycle. Once you get it, it gets easier and easier. If possible, try to learn to use your MAGIC EYE in a quiet, meditative time and place. It is difficult for most people to first experience deep vision while otherwise preoccupied in the distracting pinball machine of life. While others teach you, or watch as you try, you're likely to feel foolish and suffer from performance anxiety. Although MAGIC EYE is great fun at work and other entertaining social situations, those are not often the best places to learn. If you don't get it in two or three minutes, wait until another, quieter time. And, if it's hard for you, remember, the brain fairy did not skip your pillow. For most people, it's a real effort to figure out how to use the MAGIC EYE. Almost all of them tell us the effort was well worth it!

In all of the images in MAGIC EYE, you'll note a repeating pattern. In order to "see" a MAGIC EYE picture, two things must happen. First, you must get one eye to look at a point in the image, while the other eye looks at the same point in the next pattern. Second, you must hold your eyes in that position long enough for the marvelous structures in your brain to decode the 3D information that has been coded into the repeating patterns by our computer programs.

There are two methods of viewing our 3D images: Crossing your eyes and diverging your eyes. Crossing your eyes occurs when you aim your eyes at a point between your eyes and an image; diverging your eyes occurs when your eyes are aimed at a point beyond the image.

All of our pictures are designed to be seen by diverging the eyes. It is also possible to see them with the cross-eyed method, but all the depth information comes out backward! (If you try it, we can guarantee that you will not come out backward too.) If we intend to show an airplane flying in front of a cloud, using the diverging eye method, you will see an airplane-shaped hole cut into the cloud if you look at it with the cross-eyed method. Once you learn one method, try the other. It's fun, but most people do better with one or the other. We think that most people prefer the diverging method.

Another common occurrence is to diverge the eyes twice as far as is needed to see the image. In this case, a weird, more complex version of the intended object is seen. (By the way, if you diverge your eyes while looking at yourself in a mirror, you can find your "third eye" . . . at least we were told that in a letter we received. But you must spend several hours a day looking at yourself in a mirror. Remember, we said it was all right.)

One last note before you start. Although this technique is safe, and even potentially helpful to your eyes, don't overdo it! Straining will not help, and could cause you to feel uncomfortable. That is not the way to proceed. Ask your nephew or the papergirl to give you some help; they'll probably be able to do it in ten seconds. The key is to relax and let the image come to you.

METHOD ONE

Hold the image so that it touches your nose. (Ignore those who might be tempted to make comments about you.) Let the eyes relax, and stare vacantly off into space, as if looking through the image. Relax and become comfortable with the idea of observing the image, without looking at it. When you are relaxed and not crossing your eyes, move the page slowly away from your face. Perhaps an inch every two or three seconds. Keep looking through the page. Stop at a comfortable reading distance and keep staring. The most discipline is needed when something starts to "come in," because at that moment you'll instinctively try to look at the page rather than looking through it. If you look at it, start again.

METHOD TWO

The cover of this book is shiny; hold it in such a way that you can identify a reflection. For example, hold it under an overhead lamp so that it catches its light. Simply look at the object you see reflected, and continue to stare at it with a fixed gaze. After several seconds, you'll perceive depth, followed by the 3D image, which will develop almost like an instant photo!

The last pages of this book provide a key that shows the 3D picture that you'll see when you find and train your MAGIC EYE.

There are some images in the book that do not contain a hidden picture; instead the various repeated objects will seem to float in space at different distances when viewed correctly. These images are on pages 21 and 29. For many, they are easier to see than the other pictures.

We wish you luck, and hope you enjoy this fantastic new art form!

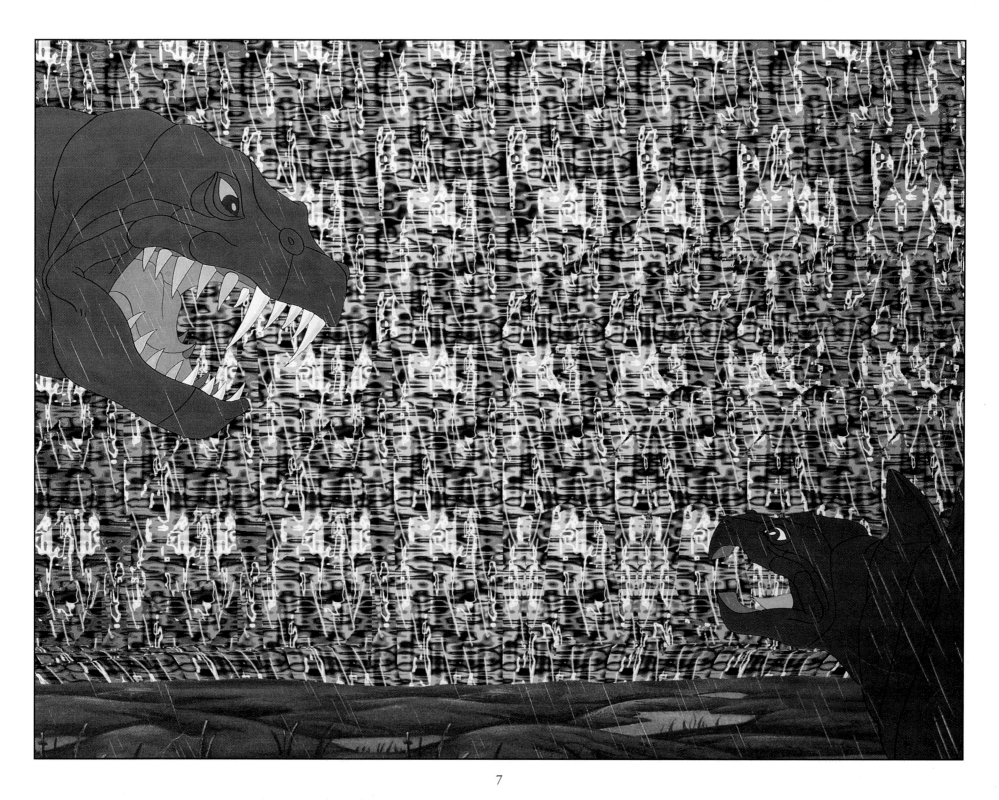

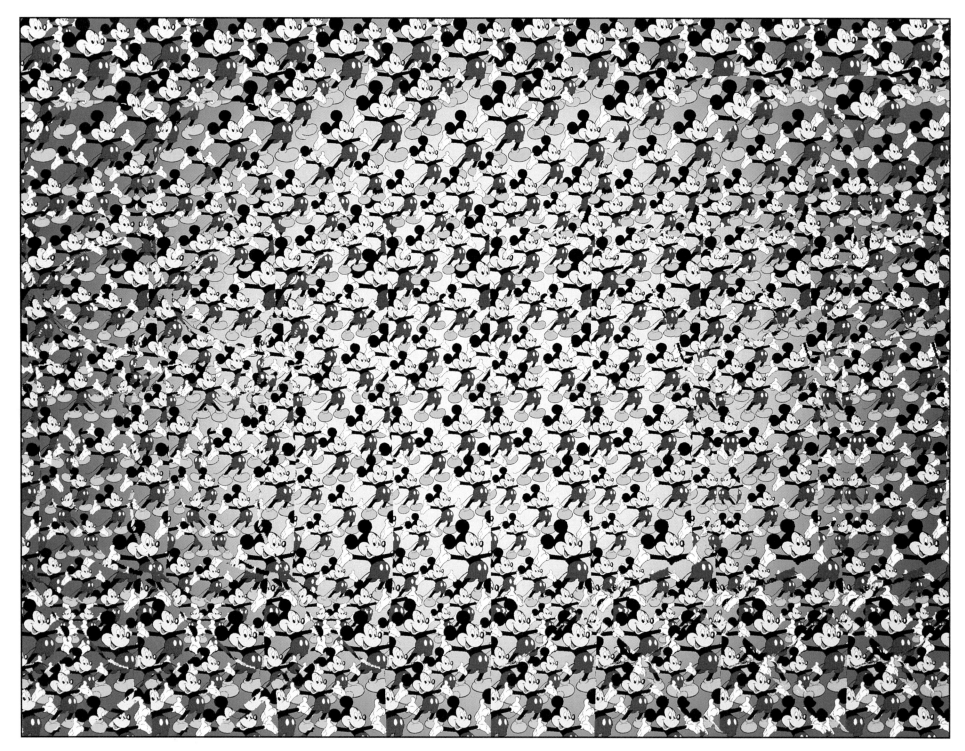

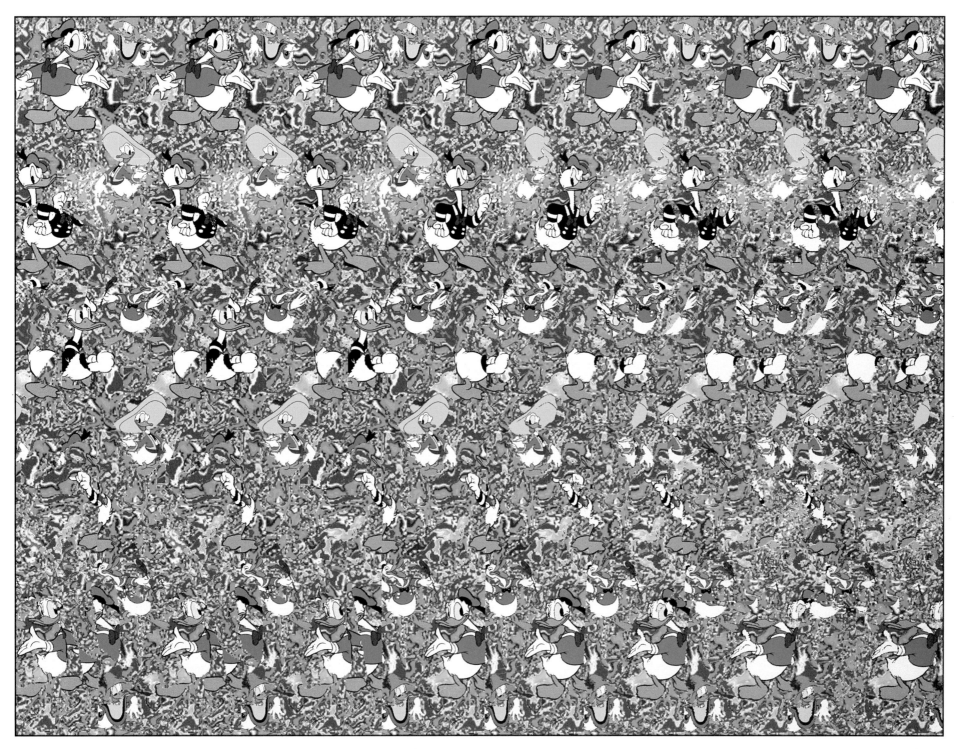

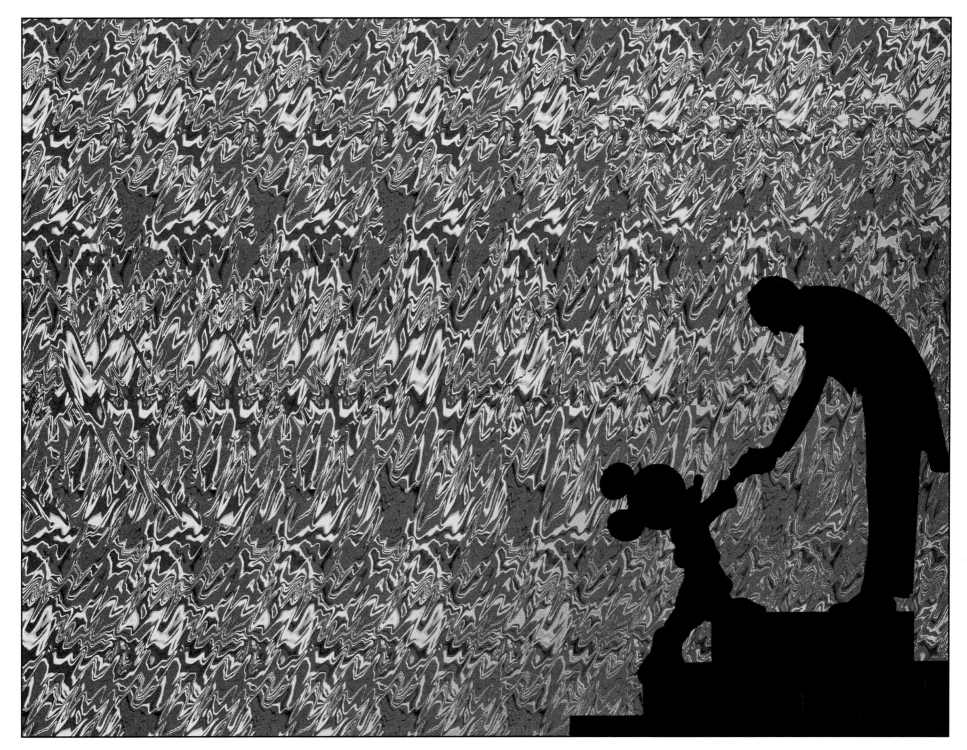

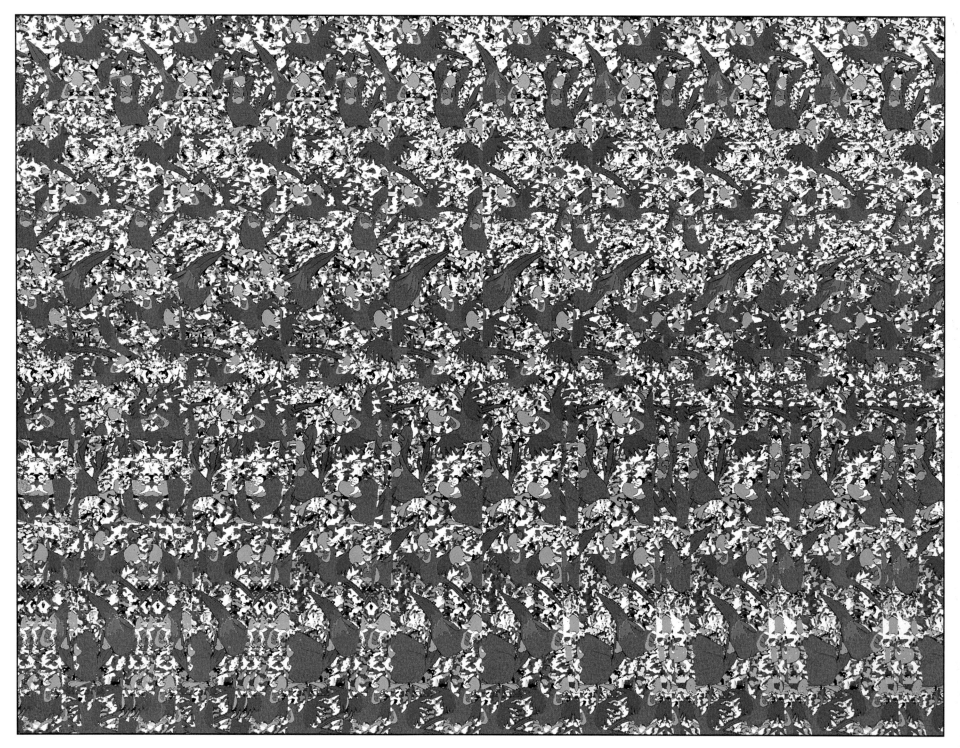

12

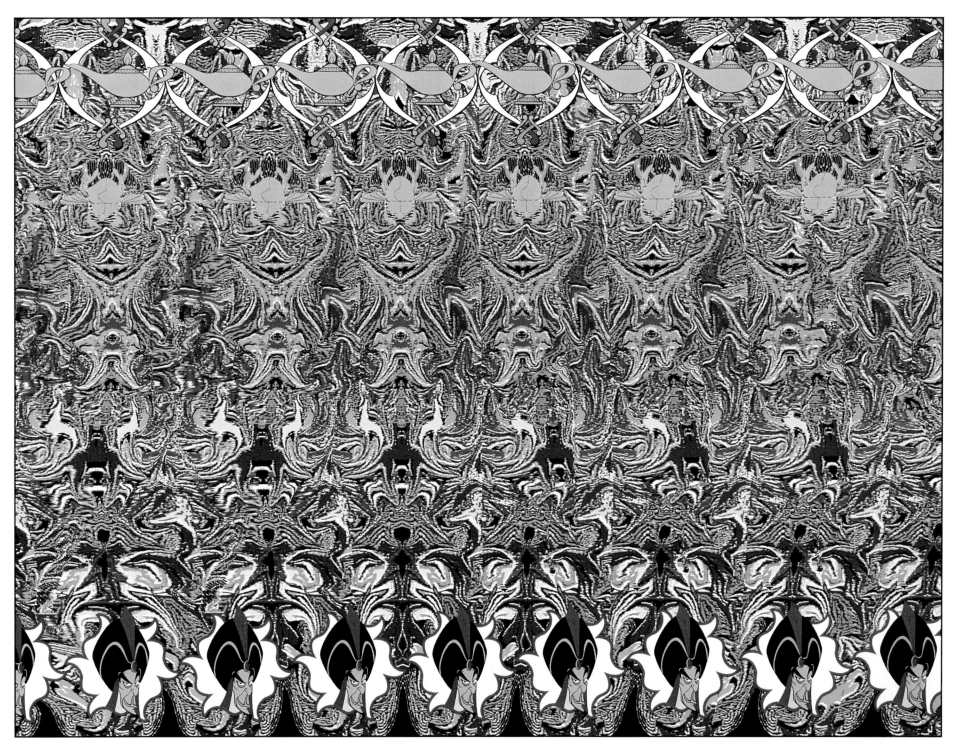

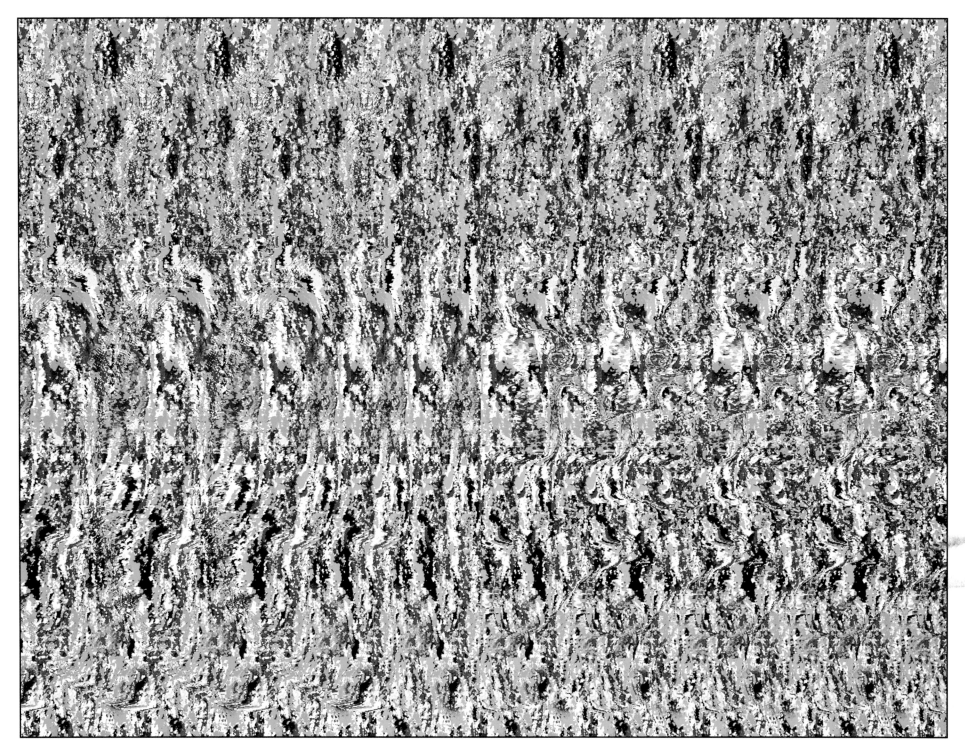

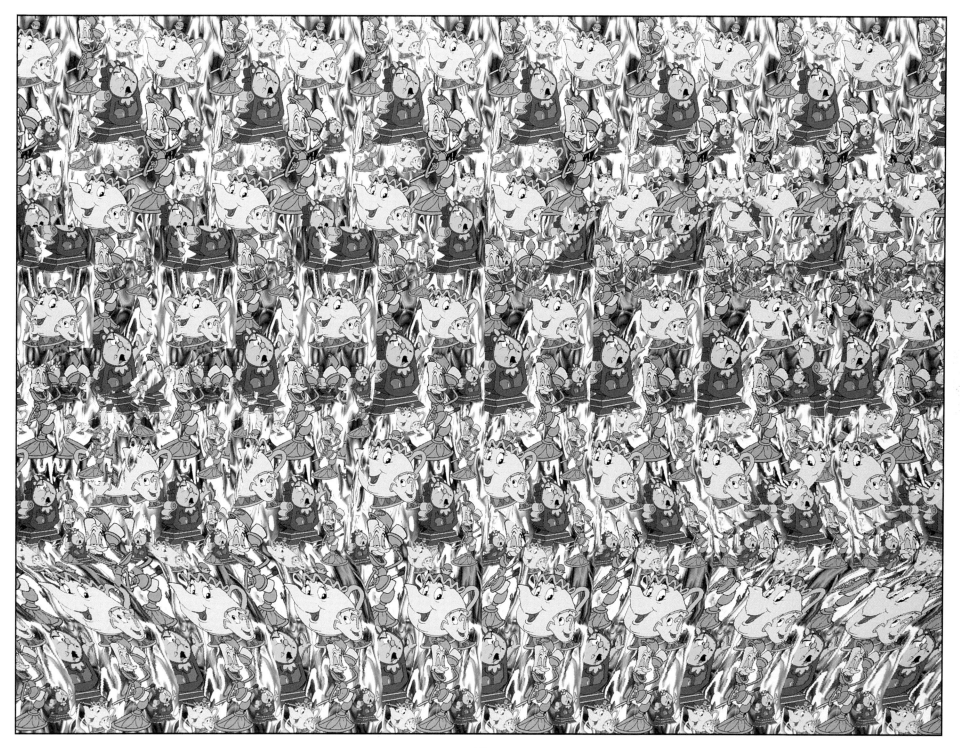

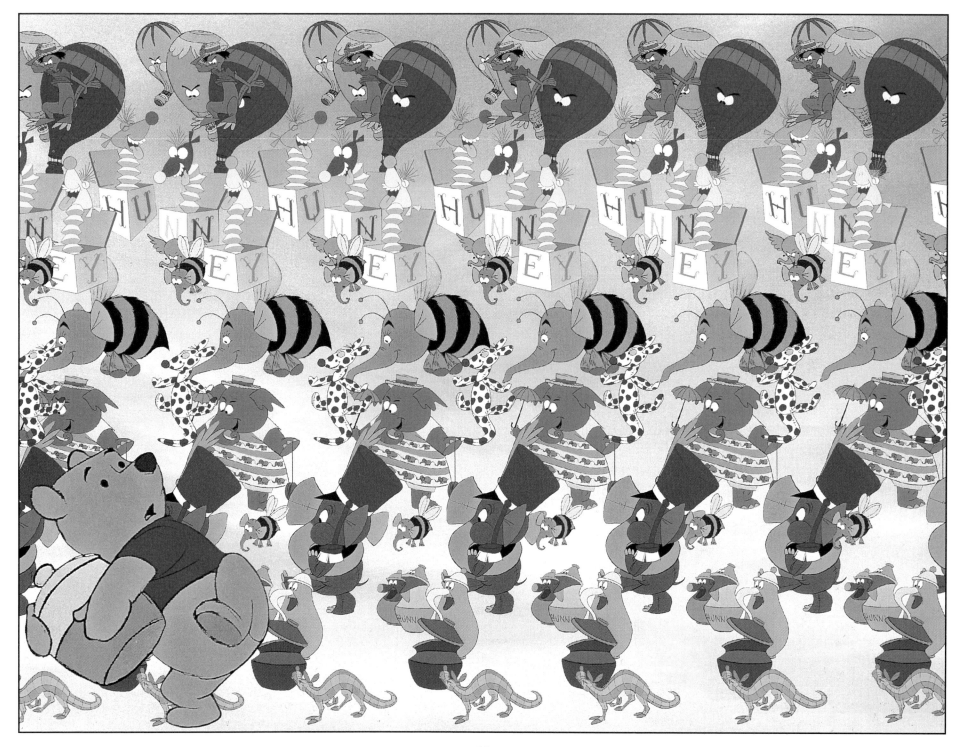

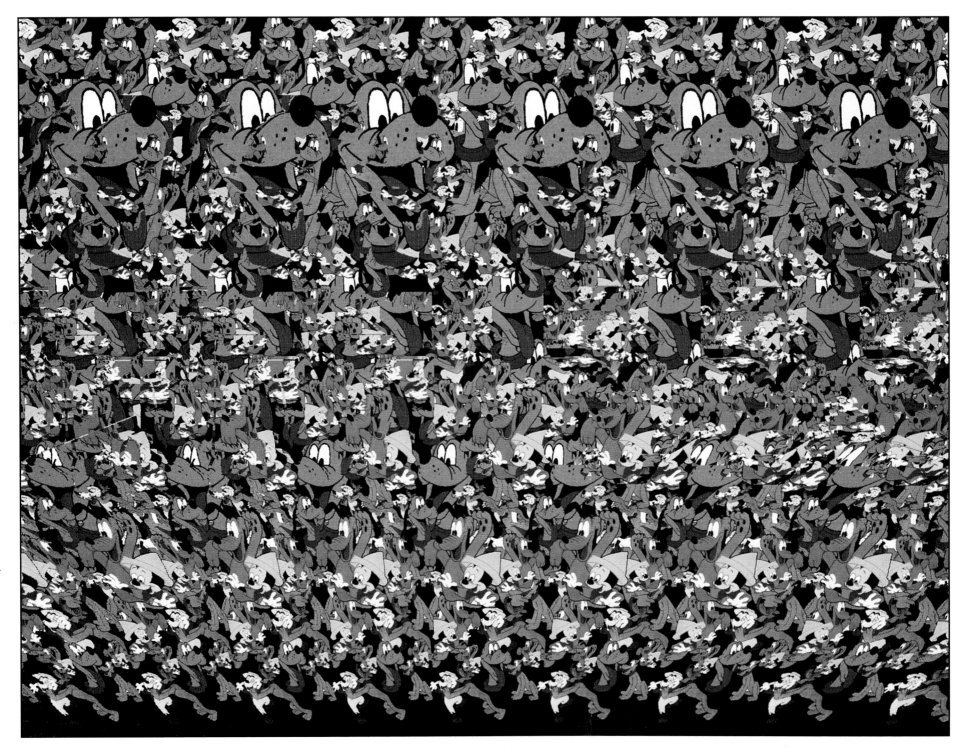

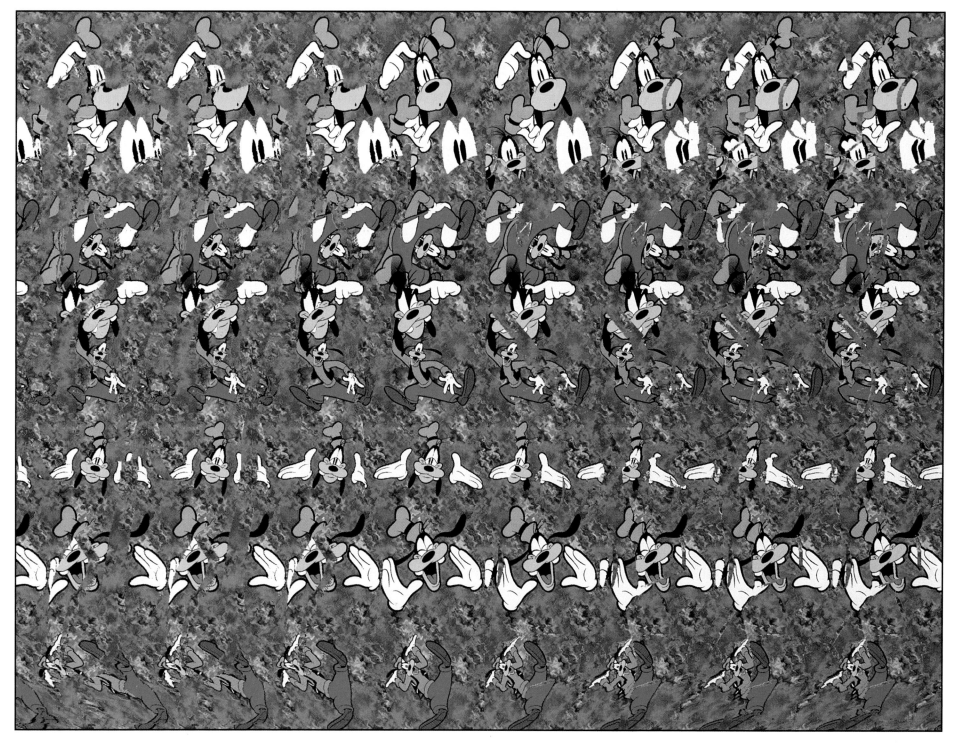

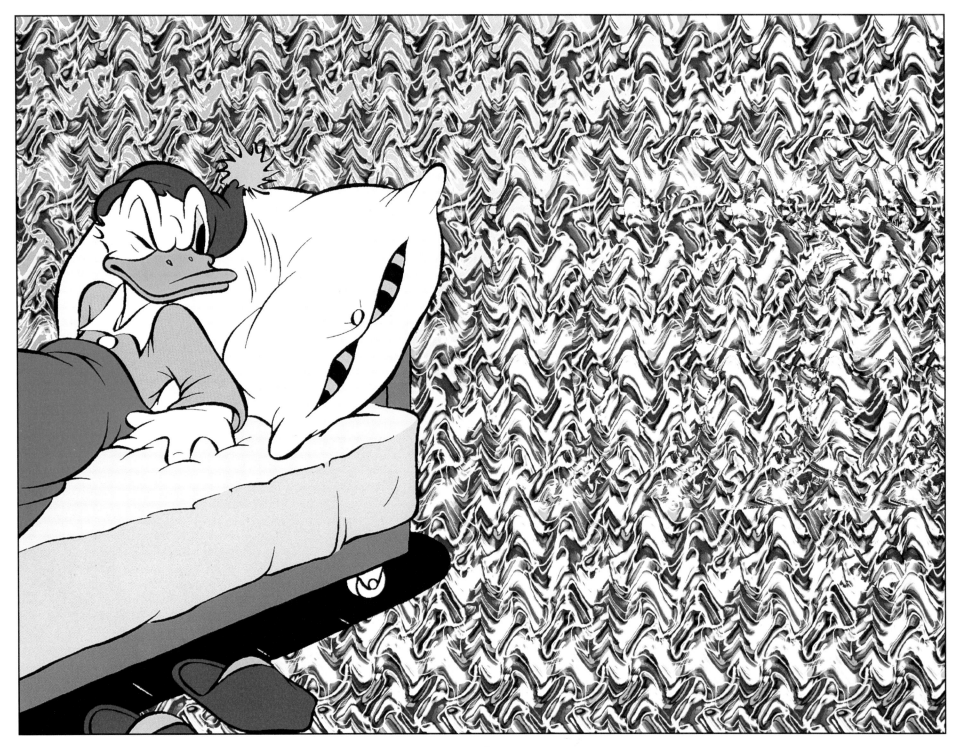

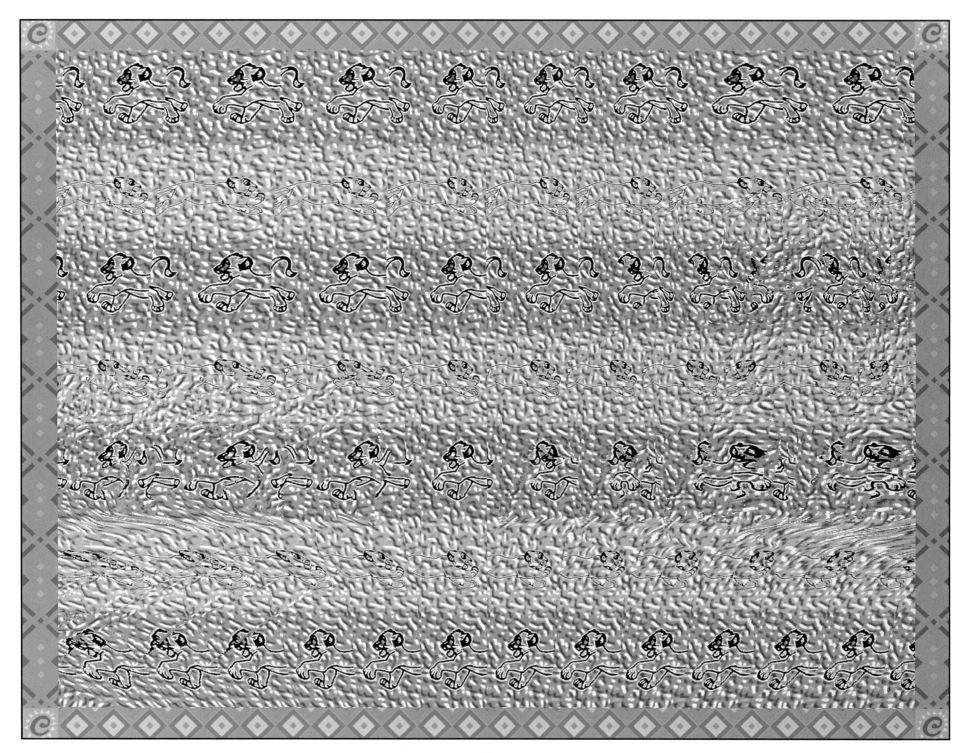

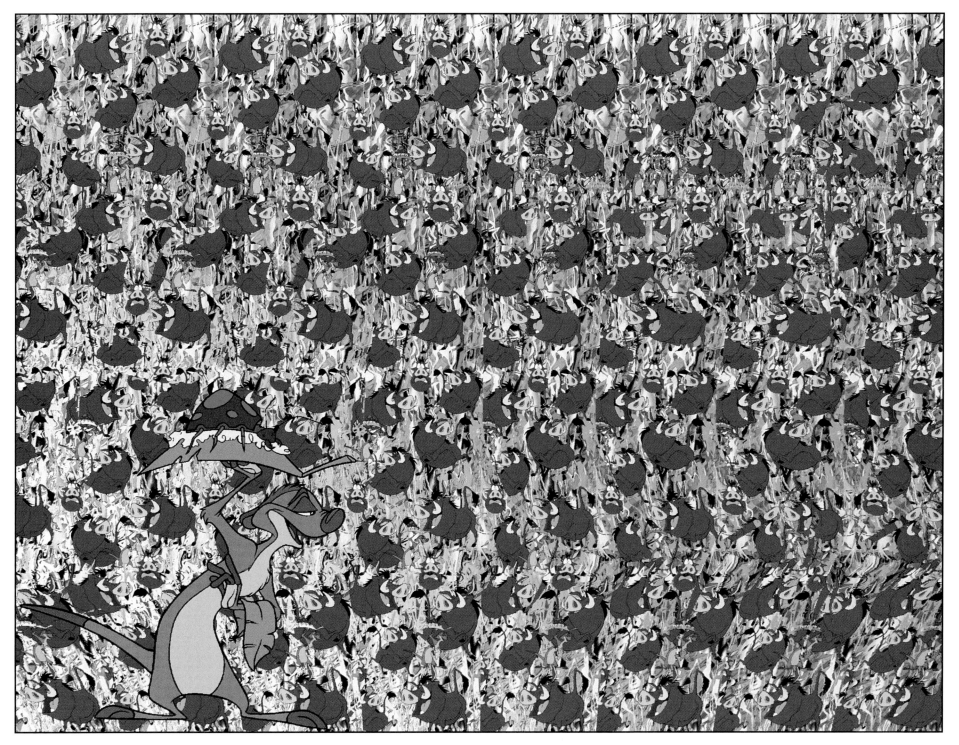

p. 5 Pirate Ship
(Peter Pan)

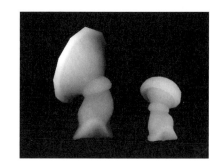

p. 6 Mushroom Dancers
("The Nutcracker Suite," *Fantasia*)

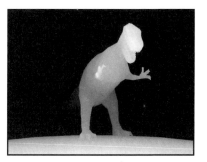

p. 7 Dinosaur
("The Rite of Spring," *Fantasia*)

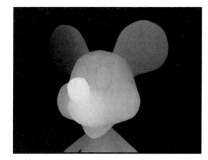

p. 8 Mickey Mouse

p. 9 Donald Duck

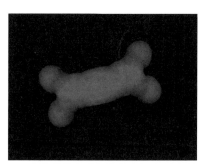

p. 10 Bone
(One Hundred and One Dalmatians)

p. 11 Horn
(Fantasia)

p. 12 Jafar
(Aladdin)

p. 13 Cave of Wonders
(Aladdin)

p. 14 The Genie
(Aladdin)

p. 15 Magic Lamp
(Aladdin)

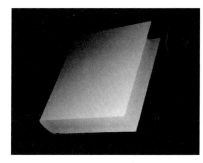

p. 16 Book
(Beauty and the Beast)

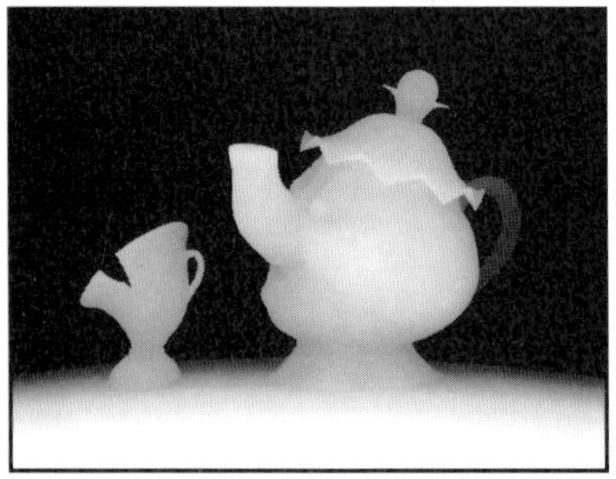

p. 17 Mrs. Potts and Chip
(Beauty and the Beast)

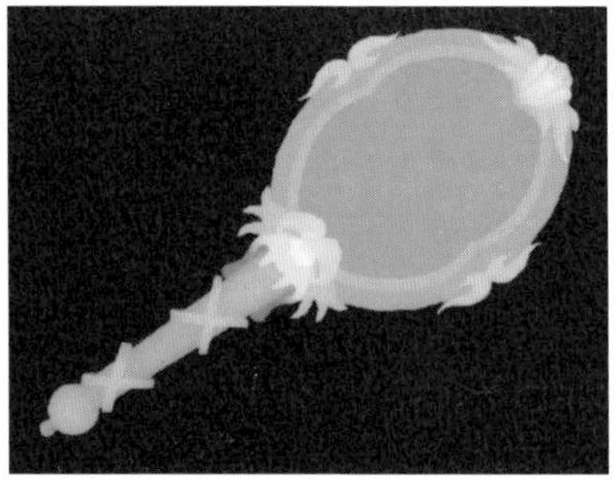

p. 18 Enchanted Mirror
(Beauty and the Beast)

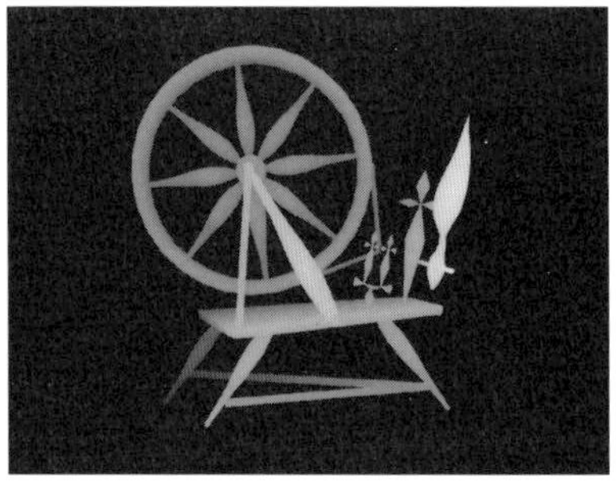

p. 19 Spinning Wheel
(Sleeping Beauty)

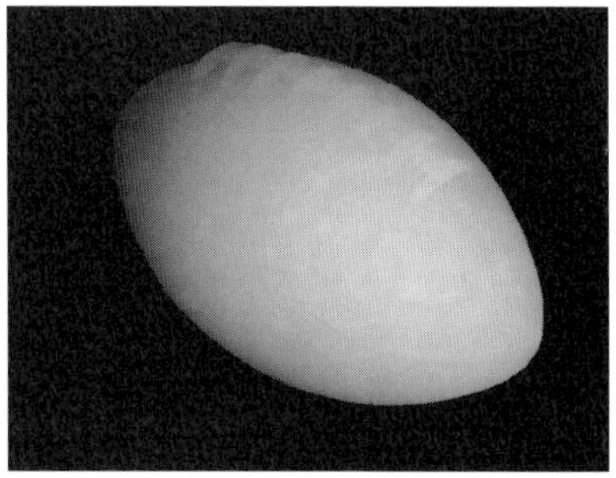

p. 20 Football
p. 21 (No image)

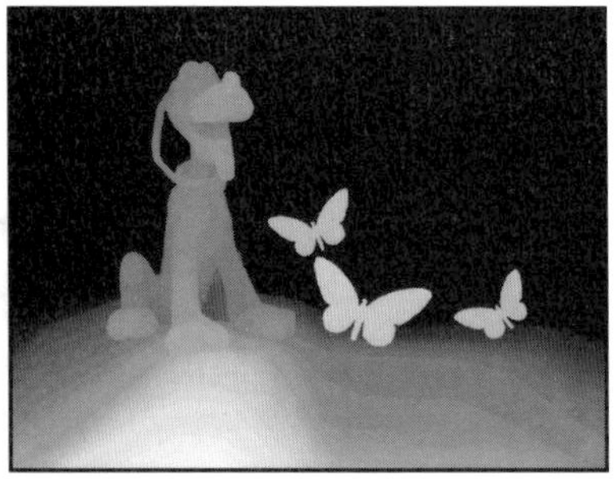

p. 22 Pluto

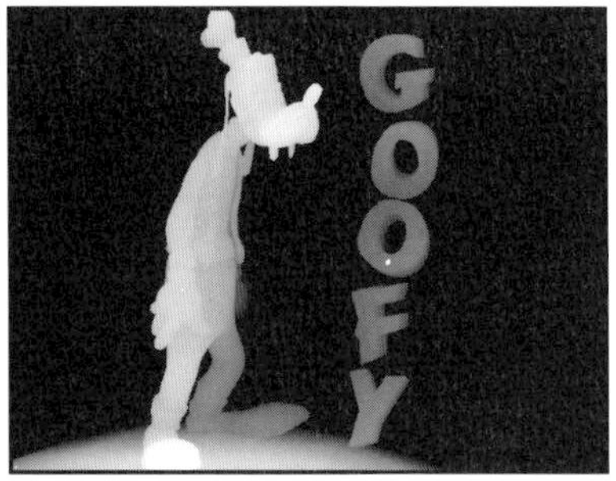

p. 23 Goofy

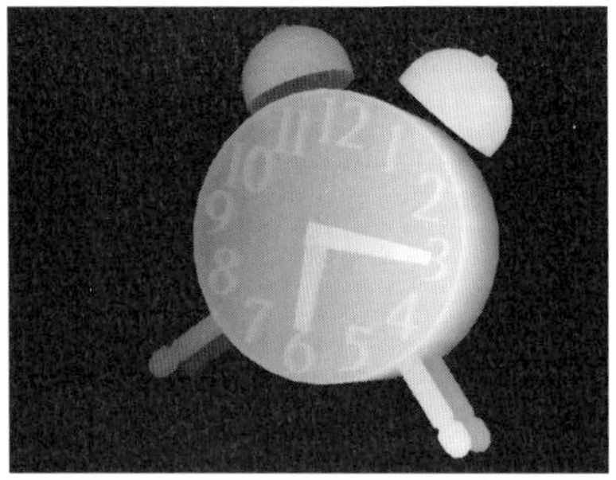

p. 24 Clock

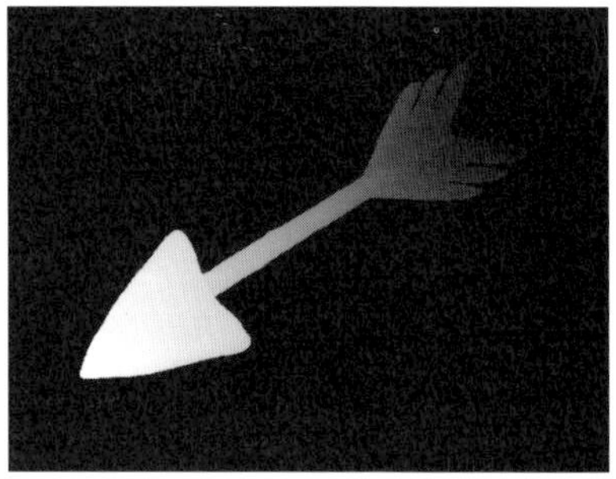

p. 25 Arrow
(Robin Hood)

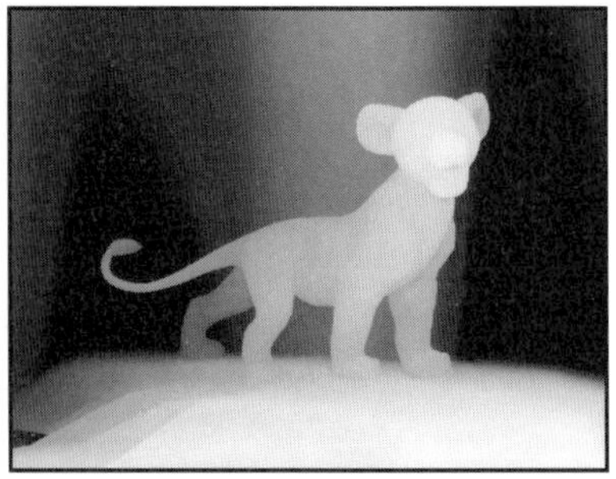

p. 26 Simba
(The Lion King)

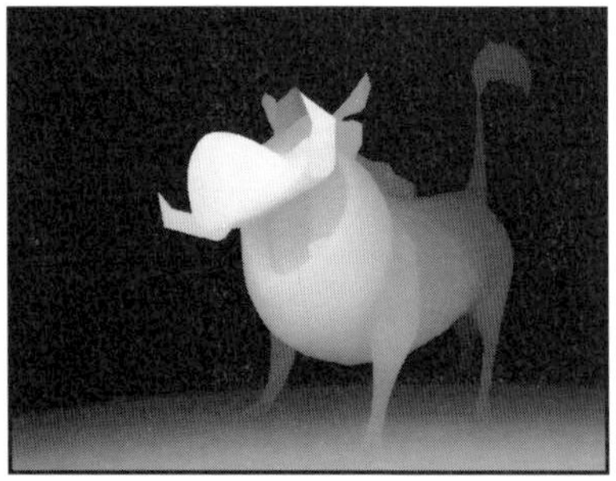

p. 27 Pumbaa
(The Lion King)

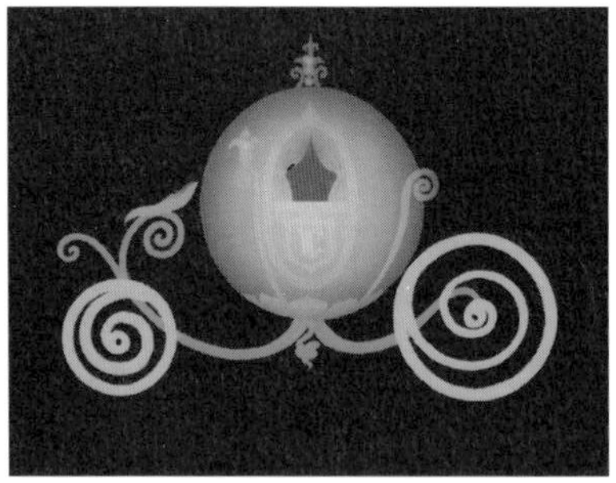

p. 28 Pumpkin Coach
(Cinderella)
p. 29 (No image)

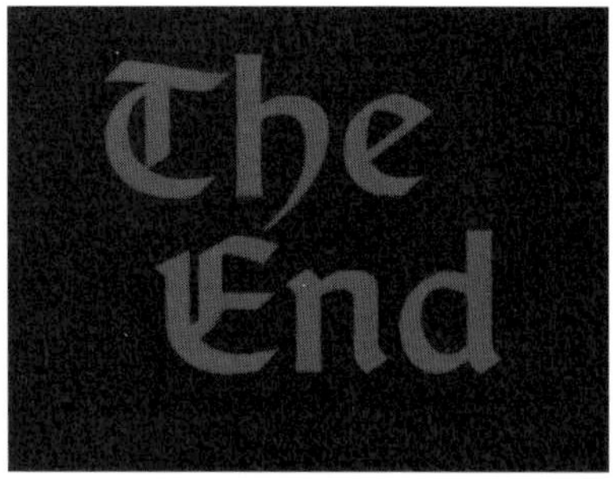

p. 30 The End
(Snow White and the Seven Dwarfs)

OVER NIGHT BOOK

This book must be returned before the
first class on the following school day.

DATE DUE

9·5·97			
9·16·97			
10·1·97			
10-3-97			
10·9·97			
10·30·97			
10·31·97			
MAR 1 4 2002			
OCT 2 9 2002			
GAYLORD			PRINTED IN U.S.A.

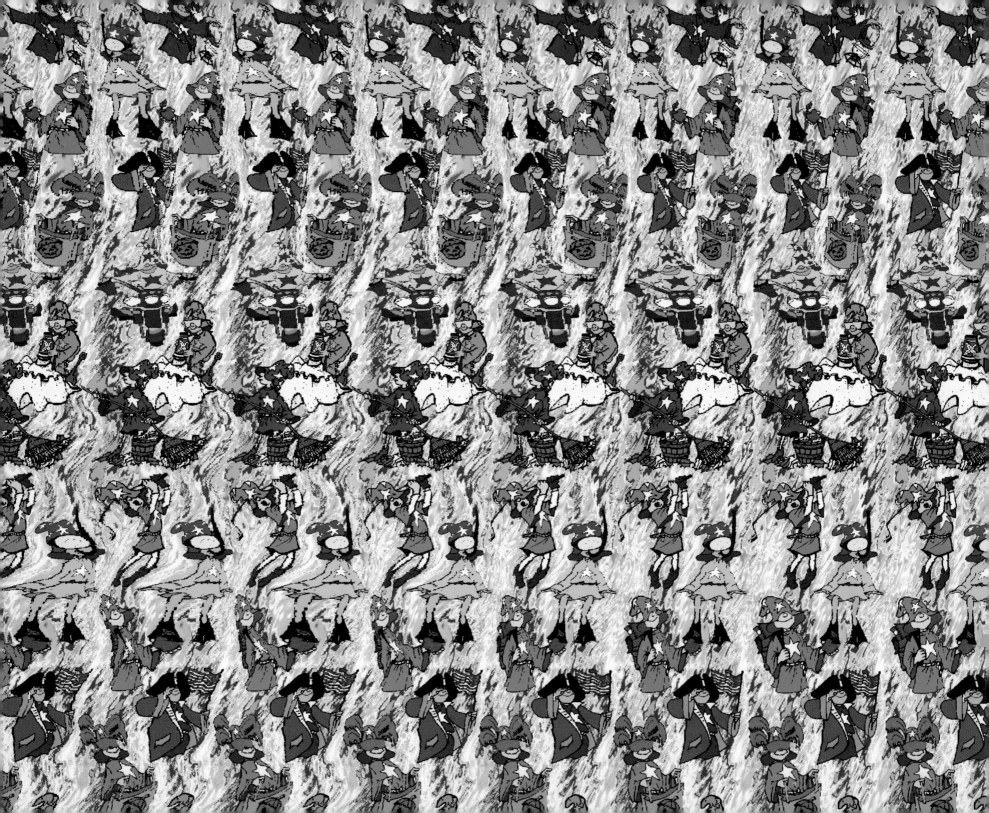